CHARISMA'S HOMECOMING

DAKIARA

MIND FLOW PUBLISHING & PRODUCTION LLC

First Printing: 2019

ISBN 978-1-951271-02-2 Paperback

ISBN 978-1-951271-03-9 Ebook

Additional copies of this book and others are available by mail or by visiting the website listed below. Check website for pricing.

Mind Flow Publishing & Production LLC

PO Box 48768 Cumberland, North Carolina 28331-8768

www.mindflowpublishingproduction.com

Cover design by Carrie & Co.

Editing by Stories Matter Editing

Formatting Design by Turbo Kittens Industries

Thank you for helping to bring Charisma to life......

DEDICATION

TO MY LOVES
DAQUAN, DEJA, DANTE
KEVONN AND KIARA

RIP
DAQUAN JAMIQUE 95
&
KIARA DENISE 00
Special Thanks
To GOD for Giving Me
The Strength and The Words
To Do This Project.
Blessed by The Experiences to Draw From
It Has Not Always Been Easy.
Dedicated to Some Who Have Gone Before Me

Mary Merriman

Naomi Thompson

1

THE GREAT ESCAPE

Never did she imagine in a million years she would be here and raising a child in her hometown, a town that she had left behind many years before. Much less one that wasn't even hers. It was if all her fears had somehow become reality in the blink of an eye.

Charisma was the product of the foster care system and her childhood had been anything but fun. She had been bounced around from family to family, eight to be exact, within as many years. At seventeen, she ran away from Polkton, Iowa and never looked back, that is until now. After fifteen years she has been forced to come back to take care of some "family business" she never knew she had. For as long as she could remember, she had been alone in this world and she had always been fine with that. Her mother had succumbed to cancer when she was eight. She had watched her mother suffer for several years from the ravages of the disease, but she knew that she couldn't fight any longer. They couldn't locate her father, he left right after she was born. Charisma never really knew who he was or much about him. He could have been standing right beside her and never would have known it. As a child she often fantasized that

1

was the case and that he would come in and save her from any of the foster families she was stuck with. It never happened. He never came to claim her. He never came to save her from the torment some put her through. She made up her mind that as soon as she could she was going to get away and never look back. She was going to show them all she could make it on her own. As soon as she graduated high school, two days later she was gone like a whisper in the wind. She had saved enough money for a bus ticket to New Orleans. She knew no one was going to come looking for her, and they wouldn't think about looking there even if they did. She remembered her mom talking about that place once. The music, the atmosphere, and the people it was completely different from Iowa that was for sure. Her mom had visited it once and her face always seemed to light up with the remembrance of all the fond memories, especially when she spoke of Bourbon Street. It seemed to be a great place to get a new start in life.

Charisma had meticulously planned this move for some time, and she was determined to never come back to Polkton. During Charisma's last year of school, she got a job working at Walton's Pharmacy. A customer came in and was talking about a trip she was planning to take soon. She herself had planned it out for over a year. The customer had watched to see if prices fluctuated or if one time of year was better to travel than others. Charisma began planning at that moment. She knew she was going to be taking the bus, it was cheaper. She began watching and checking prices and the schedules. She knew she would be graduating on a Saturday, so Monday she would be on the first bus out. With watching the bus prices, they didn't fluctuate the same as airplane tickets. Charisma wanted to make sure she had enough money to find a place and pay rent for at least 6 months in case it took her a while to find a job. She began looking up apartments as well as hotel prices just in case it took a bit to find a place. Her plan went off without a hitch; she left and never looked back. She kept in contact with only two of her childhood friends, Jackson and Olivia. Those two knew everything about her, the good along with all the bad that had happened. Unfortunately, there was a lot of bad during those years. They kept all her secrets. Although not all the foster homes were bad, the first two were great in fact, but those two families couldn't keep her. The first ended up having their own child and the second the father died, and so they were forced to move away. The third family simply wanted to receive a check; they didn't even have a place for her to sleep so by the time the caseworker did the first home visit they pulled her out. She went on to the fourth home, she lasted there for two and a half years, that was the longest. This family was nice until the mother, Madison remarried, and the new father tried to touch her and the other daughter Naomi, who was five. She told her caseworker who removed her and all the other children from the home. Being from a small town there was always someone gossiping.

Mrs. Madison, although she claimed she was a devout Christian couldn't help talking about the incident with her women's group. "The nerve of that girl, I opened up my home to her like the good Christian I am."

The rest of the ladies all chimed in and agreed. By this time word was spreading around town that Charisma was a bad apple to have around, and it was even said she was coming on to the men and the boys in the home. The fifth and sixth families, she was there for about a year and a half a piece. Both families had drug addicts for parents, but somehow they kept passing inspection when the caseworker would come for the home visits. She tried to give hints about what was going on in the home, she even had her friends call in with anonymous tips, but nothing. Charisma just did as she was told and waited until she was pulled from the home and moved to the next.

She tried her best to not cause any trouble, but she always

felt it coming, like an approaching thunderstorm. The family started doing things without her. She felt like an outcast. The caseworker visited more frequently and always seemed to have someone with her. One of the people was Ann Sanders. She was the mother of family number seven. She was moved to family seven right when she turned sixteen. That was where she met Adrian. He was their biological child. Although he was supposed to be her foster brother, she found him very attractive and it became apparent that he thought the same of her. It wasn't long before Adrian's mother caught them kissing. She liked Charisma, so she told her she would give her another chance but if it happened again, she had to go. Charisma obeyed the rule of not being alone with Adrian and attempted to keep those feelings away.

As a 16-year-old young lady looking for love from anyone who showed her attention. Adrian would smile and tease her incessantly; he often would push her hair from her face with his fingertips. Charisma managed to not be alone with Adrian, she even stopped looking at him altogether. Adrian however did not keep up his end of the bargain. One day when his mother was late coming home from work, he decided he would try to see how far he could go with Charisma. Things got out of hand and the next thing she knew, he was trying to rape her. Luckily, his mom came in before he could get too far. But instead of helping Charisma, the story was twisted around to make Adrian look like he was the victim. Like with a lot of her previous families, she always got dealt the bad end of the stick.

Adrian's mom Ann told her, "If you ever tell anyone about this, I will say you came on to him. You are just a foster kid; who you think they will believe?"

At that time Adrian was playing football for the local high school and he was pretty good. His mom didn't want anything hurting his chances at a scholarship. Ann called the case worker that night, so Charisma could be placed in her eighth and final home.

Ann told Janie, the caseworker that Charisma just wasn't getting along with her son. She said she tried to keep her as long as she could, but it just wasn't working out. Janie was a middle-aged woman who was good at her job, she herself had 4 children, and knew how tough it could be raising them all. Janie had inherited Charisma's case from Samantha who was fresh out of college and became burned out by cases like Charisma's where the system seemed to fail those who needed their help the most. Samantha ended up having a nervous breakdown because she felt she had let Charisma and others down. Janie welcomed the challenge Charisma presented, every time she had met with her, there was something in her eyes, showing her innocence. Janie knew just the place for her to go for her final foster placement.

Charisma was beginning to think that the world was against her. She was finally placed with Ms. Beatrice, a 62-year-old lady who could barely care for herself much less for a seventeen-year-old. She made the decision right then and there that her senior year was going to be as quiet and uneventful as she could make it and as soon as she graduated, she was going to make a fresh start. It was important for her to graduate because that was something her mom didn't do, and her mom always stressed the value of education to her, especially as she got sicker and sicker. She made Charisma promise to always do her best even if she didn't go to college and to make sure she graduated high school. She intended to keep that promise. The last year of high school passed with a breeze, she got a job at the local drug store a few days a week and saved up her money. Ms. Beatrice didn't have any trouble out of her at all. She began seriously planning her escape and purchased her ticket four months before graduation so that she wouldn't chicken out. Olivia and Jackson tried to talk her out of it a time or two, but it didn't work. Olivia was her oldest and dearest friend. Charisma met her when she was in her second home. Olivia lived 5 houses down. She introduced Charisma to Jackson when she was moved to her third home. From that point on they were all thick as thieves. They knew when she purchased the ticket that it was a done deal. There was going to be no stopping her. Charisma's mind was made up. She had even called a few Walton's Pharmacies in nearby towns to inquire if they were hiring so she could transfer her information over once she got there. And just as she had planned two days after graduation, she boarded the bus for New Orleans and had never looked back. She called 2003 the year of her re-birth.

2

ON HER OWN

Twelve years had passed, and all has been well with Charisma since moving to New Orleans. She found herself a home. The people received her kindly, and she finally felt as if she found a place that she truly belonged Charisma soaked up the creole music and vibrant cultural scene in New Orleans. She participated in a few second lines. They were hyped up the entire 8 blocks. Charisma had so much fun. She could tell why her mom fell in love with it here. The music and the food were so rich and colorful. It seemed as if everyone was always in a happy mood. This wasn't what she was used to, but she loved every minute of it. The only thing she wasn't used to were the storms and hurricanes that came through with such force. There were so many in the years since her arrival in Louisiana. One of the most damaging storms ever to hit that area was Katrina. That was almost enough to make her pack it up and head back to Iowa. The apartment she was living in withstood a lot of damage. It flooded and the roof was blown clear off. The winds were in excess of 120 miles per hour at times. Charisma watched in horror as a car door was snatched off the vehicle and the door hit one of her neighbors.

She was on top of another neighbor's home and had to be rescued by boat. The water was so high; there were alligators and a few snakes swimming about in the streets. All of this was foreign to Charisma, it seemed like it was a bad movie, but she was living it. The damage she witnessed wasn't even the bad part. Compared to most she was very fortunate. So many people lost their lives. She had to leave for a bit but was finally able to return. That is when she met Tyrese St. Vincent. She had no interest in getting truly involved in a serious relationship, she was just tired of doing things alone. The hurricanes truly scared her. Sure, she had a few friends, well more like acquaintances really. Olivia and Jackson would never forgive her if she got too attached to anyone else.

But with Tyrese it was different, something seemed to have clicked in her soul when their eyes first met. She knew she stared a little too long the first time, because their gaze locked and for some odd reason neither one wanted to let go. They just stood there and smiled.

A customer finally interrupted them by asking for some directions to the baby diapers aisle, Charisma walked him to the aisle. She was thankful for the intervention. That was the first time anyone had made her react like that ever in her life. At the age of thirty she realized she had never experienced true love, or just love period, from anyone other than her mom and her two friends. Her mind was jumping ahead in leaps and bounds, she knew this and besides she would probably never see this guy again after all New Orleans is a huge city, he was probably just a tourist passing through.

Caught off guard and deep in her thoughts, Tyrese walked up to Charisma, and introduced himself. "Hello, my name is Tyrese, and you are?"

Stuttering, she managed to get out "Ch...Cha...Charisma, it is a pleasure to meet you. What can I help you with today?"

Tyrese simply smiled. "Your number for starters would be nice but I won't press the issue. There will be plenty of time for that. What I would like, is to know everything I can about you. But I somehow think this isn't the time or place. Are you free this evening?"

Charisma smiled and nodded yes.

"Good, pick any place you would like to go and tell me I'll have the pleasure of your company at dinner this evening, so we can start writing the beginning of our story."

Charisma immediately thought of Giovanni's, it was exclusive, and she knew it would be hard to get in there without a reservation, but he did say pick anywhere didn't he? She told him the place and the time, and he agreed without hesitation. He turned on his heels and began to walk away, walked two steps and turned back around and confirmed the time just once more. She nodded yes. He continued to leave. The bells above the door chimed merrily as the door closed behind him. She realized she had been holding her breath the entire time. Charisma finally exhaled, as her mind began to wander. She felt a smile creep to her face, and she experienced a calm deep within her soul. It was kind of a weird feeling for her. Being alone had hardened her heart and dulled it to some advances from would be suitors. Through the rest of her shift, she thought about the guy who managed to make her a little nervous and giddy inside.

The rest of Charisma's evening went well at work and once she got home she contemplated showering and going to bed but she remembered the handsome man she met earlier at her job and the fact they had a dinner date in about an hour. There was no way he was going to be able to get reservations on such short notice, Giovanni's was the most prestigious restaurant in New Orleans, and it managed to stay packed. She wished she would have gotten his number, she could have called and cancelled but now she was going to have to go and see in person the fact they won't be able to get in and that will be embarrassing for everyone involved. Charisma's thoughts drifted off into the direction of her past.

3

THOUGHTS OF THE PAST

She had met several men in her twelve years here and even dated a few; there was Remy, Stephen, and Marcus St. Claire. They were all handsome and charming in their own way but none of them lasted, and none were serious. Marcus and Remy wanted more than what she could give at the time, and she wasn't about to compromise her beliefs for any man. Stephen was, well, he just was the bad version of them all. He was jealous and controlling and she didn't want that kind of presence in her life. It had taken her five years to start dating once she arrived in Louisiana and that was when she met Remy LeMare. He was just as dreamy as his name implied. His family was one of the wealthiest in New Orleans, but that never mattered to Charisma. She wasn't impressed by those who had money, she never had it and had gotten by just fine. Remy introduced her to the folklore of NOLA They often went and hung out with the fortunetellers and voodoo priestess. Remy was obsessed with communicating with his deceased twin brother Jacob. He had died when they were six, in a terrible boating accident and Remy blamed himself. At first, Charisma was enchanted by this mystical world, but it didn't take long before it began to make her a little paranoid about some things. In the beginning she thought maybe she could speak to her mom again. Oh, how she missed her so.

As she saw Remy's obsession grow, she knew that was not the way for her to go. She knew her mom was watching over her. Charisma would occasionally have dreams about her mom. The way the dreams unfolded a voodoo priestess from the French Quarter named Madame Tessa, told her that her mom was trying to warn her of impending danger. She even went so far as to tell her that her mother sensed danger in dealing with a man. Charisma began feeling chills shortly thereafter when waking up from those dreams. She would feel them again when she was around Remy.

She began distancing herself from Remy and by the time he noticed, it had been several months. Charisma used that as the reasoning behind the breakup. Simply that he stopped noticing her. He didn't like it, but he let her go without a fight. He even apologized and said he just had to fight the demon inside, which was the guilt of his brother's death. It was supposed to have been him in the water, they had switched places at the last minute just before the tragedy struck. He always thought it was funny to pull the switcharoo on their parents. The two brothers switched boats, so their parents couldn't tell them apart without getting close to them. Childish he knew, but it was their thing. Remy was never able to forgive himself. Charisma urged him to get help. He said he would. But the help never came. A few months after their breakup she read in the local paper that Remy was found dead, he died the same way Jacob had years before. His demon had finally got the best of him.

A few months later she ran into Stephen St. Thomas. She literally ran into him on her bicycle. Stephen was the boy next door, or at least Charisma thought he was. They dated a few months, again nothing serious on her part. He was completely taken with her. She noticed right away that he wanted to be around her all the time, even while she was at work. He began showing up mid-shift and just lurking around. Her boss had kindly asked him to leave a few times and she noticed Stephen got angry at the altercation. But, by the time he came to pick her up he was calm and collected once more. It was like a switch was turned on and off. Charisma wasn't experienced enough to truly understand what was going on with Stephen because she hadn't dated a lot, and she didn't expose herself to a lot of people especially since moving to New Orleans. A few weeks later, as Charisma and her boss were closing for the evening Stephen approached them from where he was lurking around the corner and accused the two of them of sleeping together. For Charisma, that was the last straw. She was willing to disregard the disruption at her job, but to blatantly accuse her of sleeping with her boss? That was it.

"Stephen, you are out of your mind. How dare you accuse Mr. James of such a thing. We are through. You need to leave." The words were spoken but they didn't seem to register with Stephen.

He looked lost for a moment. "You choosing him over me? What can he give you that I can't?"

Mr. James offered Charisma a ride home, she declined, she thought she would be okay riding her bike. Stephen may be crazy, but he would never hurt her, would he? Mr. James watched as she left on her bike, Stephen had left and went the other way. He began walking towards his car and suddenly he heard a car speed off around the corner. He heard the screeching of the tires and the sound of metal colliding. He prayed that it was not Charisma. His prayers weren't answered, however. Mr. James ran around the corner as fast as he could, only to have the breath stolen from his lungs by the scene that was unfolding in front of his face. Charisma lay unconscious on the pavement, a few feet from her bicycle, which was mangled and wedged under the car. The car had crashed into another vehicle and Stephen was also unconscious. In the distance police and ambulance sirens began blaring, signaling their arrival. Luckily, another couple was walking nearby and witnessed the whole thing. They had called the police.

Charisma awakened in the hospital two days later with a broken arm, broken pelvis, a concussion and a headache that wouldn't quit. She immediately felt a pain in her abdomen that caused her to wince. Looking around she realized where she was, she yelled out in pain. A nurse quickly entered the room and asked if she was okay.

"There is a pain in my stomach. What happened to me? Why am I here?"

The nurse was unsure of what to say. "I will be right back ma'am. I'll page a doctor to come take a look at you."

Charisma knew she was in the hospital, but she couldn't remember what had happened. Why was she here? The last thing she remembered was talking to her boss. She had said goodnight and she got on her bike to ride home. She remembered Stephen was acting crazy and she told him that it was over. Then there was a crash in the distance and then nothing but darkness. Only the crash wasn't in the distance. Stephen had run her over before crashing into another vehicle head on. This accident or attempt on her life, the doctor said would leave her with chronic pain issues from the broken pelvis for the rest of her life.

Mr. James was listed as the next of kin on all her paperwork, so he was called when she woke up. As he looked at her laying there in the hospital bed, she looked so frail and not only because of the extent of her injuries.

He didn't want to be the one to tell her what had happened, but there was no one else. "Hello Charisma, how are you feeling today?" Without waiting for a reply, he continued. "You know you are like a daughter to me and whatever you need, Joannie and I are here to help you." The look on Charisma's face was of disbelief. He kept going, "a few nights ago, when you and I were leaving the store, your guy friend Stephen went ballistic and he ran you over out of jealousy. He crashed his car and he was killed in the process. I'm not sorry for what happened to him, but I am for the damage that he did to you, dear child." A tear fell from his eye as he told her that she would never be able to bear any children of her own because of this accident. "Your pelvis is broken and there was some internal damage that they had to correct. Your pelvis will heal in a few months, but there is no guarantee that the internal damage wasn't too extensive. I hate to be the one to tell you this, but there is no one else. The doctor said they could go ahead and remove your uterus. That would help with the pain, but it would also permanently take away the chance to have a child of *your own. They don't usually like to perform hysterectomies on young women, but the decision is up to you."*

Charisma looked in horror, tears began to run down her face. "Why me!!!" Crying she managed out a stiff , "No." She passed out from the stress and the effects of the pain medication they had her on. The doctor urged James to allow her time to rest, and her body time to heal, so it could deal with the massive physical and emotional trauma she had been through.

He promised her body would heal, but it would be up to her for her mind to. "She will need to rest after the surgery until she is healed, that is the most imperative thing. There may be a slight chance she can have children, but I rather give the worst-case scenario and work back from there. I don't like to give out false hope. Then before you know it, someone wants to sue me because they couldn't give life when I said there was a minimal chance."

Mr. James understood and agreed. If it was meant to be then it would be, but for now he was in agreeance with the doctor that she needed to focus on getting better.

After some slight complications, Charisma had to stay at the hospital for a few weeks after the surgery was done to repair her pelvis. During that time, she had time to really stop and think about what had happened in the last few years. When she stayed to herself, she was fine, but as soon as she allowed someone in, all kinds of craziness ensued. First, Remy had taken his life and now Stephen inadvertently had taken his trying to harm her. But he also took something else from her that could never be replaced, the opportunity to have children of her own. Prior to this, having children wasn't a topic she had really thought much about because she really hadn't found the right one so there was no rush. But now that it was a possibility being a parent was taken from her, she felt great sadness. All she ever wanted was someone to love and to love her unconditionally. Now she would never know that. Well according to the doctor, there was a chance. She decided to leave her uterus, and deal with the pain as a reminder. Everyone she had ever cared about had been taken away from her, except for Jackson and Olivia, and that is why she left them behind. They were all she had left, and she couldn't bear to lose them. Her own father left her and her mom to fend for themselves. When Charisma was old enough to understand what happened all those years before, she felt that if she wasn't born, he might have stayed with her mom. Charisma's mom was taken, but truthfully, she wouldn't have wanted her mom to continue suffering.

Charisma continued her healing process at home; Mr. James saw to it that she had a nurse to come in and check on her throughout the day to make sure she took her meds. His wife Joannie made sure that she had something to eat for breakfast and lunch. For dinner, they ordered from La'Pierre's, four times a week. That was how she ended up meeting Marcus St. Claire. Although his family had money, they were determined he would earn his keep by working at the family restaurant to pay his way through school. Marcus didn't mind at all. His parents wanted him to be a doctor, but Marcus only wanted to paint. His father, Claude, said painting was not a respectable or stable way to support a family. Marcus didn't want to hear anything of the sort; his passion was creating art for others to love. In his defense he was quite good too.

The first time he laid eyes on Charisma he became smitten. He knew he wanted to get to know her better. He could sense hurt and pain in her eyes. Instantly, he wanted to take that all away. Charisma on the other hand had no intentions of getting involved with anyone else. Especially not after what had just happened. She sensed Marcus' interest and tried her best to divert it. At times when he was delivering her food, she was even downright mean to him, to try and get him to back off. That only served to make him want to know more. One day he summoned the courage to ask if they could just talk. Nothing more, he simply wanted to get to know her and become a friend. Although she hated to admit it, she did find him amusing. She agreed, and the next delivery day, he brought enough for two. Charisma invited him to stay and dine with her. That was the beginning of an amazing friend-ship. Marcus initially agreed that he wouldn't pursue her romanti-

cally, and that friendship would be fine, but the more he got to know her, and the more time they spent together he began to want more. Over time and once she healed, they went to the movies and out to dinner, he wanted other guys to know she was his. After many months, he finally gave up the romantic pursuit. Charisma began to miss him when he stopped calling and stopped coming by. A letter arrived a few weeks later from Paris. He had decided to leave NOLA, if he couldn't do what he loved and be with the woman he loved there was no point in being in New Orleans any longer. He wished her well, and he would always love her, that much he was sure of. Charisma rubbed her fingers across the envelope and smiled. A part of her was saddened that he had left her, but happy it didn't end with death. All this time she felt as if she was cursed somehow.

4

BACK TO REALITY

Coming back from her flashback, "Suck it up Risma, you shouldn't have given him an impossible task. You might have been able to have a nice dinner tonight and enjoyed yourself. Instead of Lord knows what you are walking into."

When Charisma arrived at Giovanni's she spotted Tyrese with ease, his smile was to die for. His teeth were pure perfection. He was waving her on to the door, signaling like she was running late, to be honest she was casually walking because she knew the date was going to be a bust. Much to her surprise, he ushered her inside.

Charisma had a lot to learn. He loved her innocence and that she wasn't well versed in the world, at least from what he could tell. Tyrese was the owner of Giovanni's, so he was beyond ecstatic when that was the one place she requested they go. That was too easy of a fix for him. Of course, he wasn't going to let her know that, it was too early in the game to reveal that kind of information. He was definitely intrigued by her; he had watched her a few times over the past few months he had been in town. The restaurant had opened about six months ago and had been a success since day one. The waitlist was backlogged for months. Tyrese couldn't be happier with the business but in his personal life, there was much to be desired.

Tyrese escorted her into Giovanni's and they were seated without any wait. She couldn't help but be impressed.

Who is this guy? She thought to herself as they made their way to a table. *He probably already had a reservation and just lucked up that I asked for this restaurant. There is no way he got us a table just like that.* The table they were seated at was in the middle of everything and was decorated a little differently than the others she noticed.

Tyrese interrupted her thoughts, "Is everything okay Charisma? Is this table okay? Would you like to sit somewhere else, I'm sure I can get us a table somewhere else, perhaps we can trade with someone."

Smiling, Charisma simply nodded. "This is all great, it is amazing in fact. I have to ask though, Tyrese, how did you pull this off? Do you know the owner or something? How did you manage to get reservations at this place, it is booked solid for months, I know this because I was going to treat myself. Nothing special just a treat me day for my mother's passing anniversary date in a few weeks. It is my way to stay close to her."

Flashing his gorgeous smile and perfect teeth, he replied "Yeah, something like that. The owner and I go way back. I called in a favor." As he said it, he felt bad for deceiving her, he didn't want to start their friendship off under false pretenses. He looked up and noticed that she was looking at him. Their gaze locks. Neither one wanting to release the other. The waiter came and inquired as to what they would like to drink. Tyrese took the liberty of ordering the house special, a specialty wine that he had purchased himself from France last month. He was sure she would love it. "Listen Charisma, I have to be honest with you. I hope you understand my reasoning for not being totally honest with you when you asked me about how I secured a reservation. This is my restaurant… that is how I was able to get the reservation so quickly. I was thrilled when you picked this place out of all the places in New Orleans for several reasons. That means this is the "it" place and now that I know your taste, if you would do me the honor of sharing another meal with me, I can show you the best cuisine in New Orleans."

All she could do was smile. At least he was honest, and oh so handsome. That was the moment she noticed his dimple. She hadn't seen it when he was at the pharmacy. He was almost too perfect to be true.

* * *

Tyrese was calling her name "Charisma, Charisma, are you okay?"

All she could do was simply smile and nod yes. She had traveled back in time to her thoughts from earlier. "I apologize I don't know where I drifted off to, well actually I do. It was some memories, that I'm not so fond of. So Tyrese, tell me more about yourself. Where did you get the concept for the restaurant and why New Orleans of all places?"

Smiling he leaned back in his chair, "Well Char, I mean Charisma, I love to cook, always have. My family has roots here in New Orleans, although I was born in New York. I have spent a lot of my life here; I even have the accent to prove it." He was glad she was asking questions that meant she was showing some interest.

Charisma continued with the typical first date questions, "Do you plan on sticking around indefinitely, or will you be going back to your family in New York? By the way what is New York like?"

Tyrese laughed at her enthusiasm and looked around "Kind of like this, but not really. New Orleans has its own beat and vibe, so does New York. Here things are more laid back, in New

York, things are faster paced. Each city has a beauty all its own though. The skyline at night is amazing. There is always something to do, so many places to eat, museums, whatever you can think of, it is there. You want to go visit someday? I will take you when you are ready."

Charisma truly believed he would if she allowed him to. The question is would she ever trust him enough? "What do you recommend from this place Tyrese? I heard the owner knows a thing or two about cooking. I wonder if he really knows his way around the kitchen." Charisma grinned cheekily. Tyrese accepted the challenge and when the waiter came back, he told him what to bring for dinner.

While waiting on dinner to arrive. Tyrese saw it as a chance to ask about her family. "Char, please excuse me for calling you that. It fits so well though."

"I don't mind, it is fine, actually my mom used to call me that sometimes when I was younger." Charisma's body tensed up and a frown made its way to her face. She seemed to have shut down in that instant. The mere thought of her mom saddened her.

Now he almost didn't want to ask, but he wanted to get to know her, so he went ahead and laid the question out there anyway. "What does your mom and dad do if I may ask? If I am being too nosey though please tell me."

"Well you are, but isn't that what people on first dates are supposed to do? My mom passed many years ago and my dad, well I don't have one of those. Not one that I claim or who claims me. It is just me I'm afraid." Instantly she hated that she said that. "Oh my god, I certainly hope you are not another crazy dude or a serial killer looking for victims with no connections because I clearly just made myself a super easy target." Shaking her head, she laughed wryly, she thought how stupid she could have been. This whole time in New Orleans she had always been on her guard, careful to never let anyone know she was alone in this world for various reasons.

Tyrese looked astonished at first, and then he chuckled uncontrollably. He thought to himself, she is so untouched, but he just didn't know how wrong he was.

She had experienced some turmoil in life, but she didn't let it define her. She started each day with a sense of awe, like it was brand new and anything could happen, just like it was intended. Some things could not be changed but the things she could, she did.

When the food came out, Charisma was amazed that it was to die for. He chose well for her and she had to admit it. She still didn't believe he could cook himself.

"Just because you know how to pick out a good meal, doesn't mean you know how to cook one."

Tyrese immediately rose to the challenge he could detect in her tone and to prove his point, he invited her over to his place the very next night, so he could cook for her. She readily accepted, surprising herself with how quickly she felt at ease in his presence. The next evening, he outdid himself with his culinary skills. This man was gorgeous to look at, smart, could cook, kept his place clean, and not to mention he had been attentive to her needs and thoughts. Charisma was waiting for something to go wrong. It always does. It always has. Tyrese didn't change up on her, if anything he became more attentive all the while running a thriving business. Even when he had to travel back and forth to New York, he made sure she knew he was thinking of her. She was falling in love with him. She held out for as long as she could, during the first year and a half she told him she wasn't trying to get into anything serious and he agreed. She hadn't expected that but was relieved. Going into the second year he asked if she would ever consider dating him officially. They were technically there already, but because of her hesitation in the beginning he never wanted to label their relationship because he didn't want to scare her away.

"Things are fine as they are, why do you want to change them Tyrese? We don't need the labels. When they start coming into play that is when things begin to change."

He looked at her with those same gorgeous greyish with a hint of green eyes and smiled that beautiful smile, "I want it all with you Char, I have been patiently waiting for you to want it all with me. Tell me you want it all with me?" Just then Charisma's phone rang... it was Olivia.

"Charisma, you need to come home. It is Ms. Beatrice she is not doing well."

Not mentally prepared to deal with that now, Charisma paused for a minute and said, "I promise, I will be home soon." Hanging up the phone she realized, she had hung up too quickly because Tyrese was still there waiting for an answer. That was back in 2017, and Charisma still hadn't made it home, and she still hadn't given Tyrese an answer to his question. For all he knew they were just friends, and she was content with that. Tyrese had tried to urge her to go home, to see about Ms. Beatrice and to see her friends.

He couldn't believe she had been in New Orleans all that time and had never returned home, not even once. His heart went out to her, he knew that had to be a lonely existence and it took so much courage to come to a place you had never been before and to start over at such a young age. But he was there now, and she would never have to deal with being alone again if he had anything to say about it. *If only she wasn't so stubborn*, he thought to himself. He wanted to marry her, settle down, and start a family. Charisma had never told him about possibly not being able to have children. Honestly, she never thought they would get this far. She had been pushing him away every chance she got, constantly keeping him at arm's length. Although she enjoyed his company, she just didn't want to get too attached.

Every time he smiled though, Jesus, give her strength. His smile was to die for. His lips were soft and smooth. She swore he melted pieces of the wall protecting her heart with each smile he threw her way. She would never admit that to him though. That would only serve as ammunition for him to think he was on the right track.

5

2018 TWENTY-EIGHTEEN

Now the year is 2018, and for years Olivia and Jackson had tried to get her to come home especially when it was time for their class reunions. They tried for the five year, and again for the ten year, but Charisma was sure that they would let it go this year. Not a chance. The nagging calls started in January to make sure she had no time to conveniently forget or make other plans. As the time for the reunion approached about a week away Olivia called and told her that Ms. Beatrice had passed and wanted to know if she would be attending the funeral because she had no other children to handle her affairs. The funny thing about that was the year that Charisma was there she thought she was just biding her time, but she was really all the lady had. She never really took the time to get to know Ms. Beatrice because all she wanted to do was get away from a place that held nothing but bad memories for her. She wasn't mean or disrespectful to Ms. Beatrice, quite the opposite really; she didn't give her much trouble at all.

"She left a will and so you really need to come and see about her affairs. She doesn't have anyone else?"

Charisma laughed to herself, she didn't have any affairs. She was 62 when I went to live with her. "What affairs are you talking about Livia? You know she was retired when I lived with her. She was old and could barely take care of herself, much less me."

Olivia agreed. "Nevertheless, you should really get home, besides that way you will be home for the reunion. I haven't seen you in years. You have Godchildren you have never seen, and they are waiting to see you. They think you are just a figment of my imagination." Charisma couldn't deny the fact it would be good to finally be back around her friends, although she promised she wouldn't go back. She did miss them so. She agreed to be there in a few days.

Tyrese had his bags packed and was ready to go with Charisma to the airport. She hadn't asked him to go, but he was hoping that by the time they reached the airport that would change, and he would be prepared.

"Char, how long are you going to be gone?" Knowing she didn't want to go in the first place he figured he would try and ask to at least get the conversation going. He couldn't believe she was riding in silence. Normally she was very talkative. "Char, are you alright? You aren't saying much. What's the matter?"

Charisma admitted she was being rather quiet. She was just wrapped up in her thoughts on going back home. About being back in the place that tried to tear her down. The place that took her mom, and her dad. "I guess I'm just nervous and a little afraid of what awaits me in Iowa. I've been gone so long. And I've lost so much while I was there."

"Charisma my love, I'm here for you always. If you want me to go with you, just say the word, and I am there."

She thought for a minute, "Would you please come with me? I was afraid to ask. I know you have your restaurant and things to attend to here. I was trying to be okay on my own, and I understand if you need to be here for work. I will be fine. I appreciate the offer, and I love you for it."

As soon as she spoke the words, she wanted to pull them back. She was waiting for his reaction, but he didn't give one. She knew he heard her.

"Char, I have my bag in the back, I was more than prepared to go with you. I was only waiting for you to ask; I didn't want to invade your space." There was silence for a moment, Charisma didn't understand, she was certain he wouldn't let an opportunity slip by where she voiced how she felt, and he didn't pounce. More importantly, how could this man always know just when she needed him the most, and have no problem coming through for her. Surprisingly he did let it go though. Tyrese fought himself hard not to react when she said the l word. He knew she was in a vulnerable place and didn't want to take advantage of the situation and hold that over her head. Even though he had waited patiently for years to hear those words, but not like this he realized. When she became his, truly his, it would be on her terms and in her time. She was worth waiting for.

As he was about to purchase his ticket, his phone rang. It was the restaurant manager. There was so much panic in her voice. Charisma could hear her almost shouting through the phone and the sounds of sirens wailing in the background. There was an emergency. The restaurant had caught on fire. Apparently one of the employees had gone and taken a smoke break in the bathroom and threw the cigarette butt in the trash receptacle without ensuring it was put out, and a fire broke out. No one was seriously hurt, but there was significant damage to the restaurant.

"Tye, please go and take care of your business, I appreciate you wanting to be here for me. Honestly, I do, but this is more important. That is your livelihood."

He smiled as he thought, *no Char, you are my business.* He

loved her more than she would ever know. He would gladly walk away from the restaurant if she ever asked him to. He had a few offers to sell over the years and he refused simply because she was there. "Char, my love I am so sorry this happened."

Charisma assured him it was okay, hugging him close, kissed him goodbye and boarded the plane, promising to call as soon as she landed.

6

GOING BACK

The four-and-a-half-hour flight was not enough time to get her nerves under control. She seemed more hesitant than ever about going home if that was even possible. What was she going for? She still didn't believe Ms. Beatrice had any affairs that needed to be tended to. Even if she did, why couldn't the county or city just do it? Don't they have services for that? Then again, the lady did take her in, and she did do the best she could by her. They really made a nice little family. Most people thought she was Ms. Beatrice's granddaughter, since they had a lot of the same features. Their eyes were the same exact hue of hazel; they both had long dark straight hair that as soon as it got wet it immediately drew up into tight coils. The only difference in their hair was that Charisma had a patch of fine golden hairs at the nape of her neck. That was something she had as far back as she could remember, she would get teased about them as a child, so she tried to keep her hair long or down enough where it couldn't be seen. Their complexion was that of a paper bag that was kissed with a little sunshine. Permanent tan is what she used to always say. It always tickled Ms. Beatrice when people said that they resembled each other. She often teased that she had one granddaughter out there somewhere. Charisma never thought much about it because she never saw any pictures of family in the house, much less any children. Come to think of it, she never saw any pictures of Ms. Beatrice from when she was younger either.

As soon as Charisma landed, her phone began to ring and vibrate from all the missed calls and messages. It was Tyrese, he just wanted to make sure she was okay. Yes, he had her flight timed out and he had already called ahead to ensure it was going to arrive on time. He couldn't help it when it came to her. He knew she was nervous about returning home. She assured him that she was good. She asked him about the restaurant and if everything was okay.

"Char, it was... well is, pretty bad. It is a little worse than I originally thought. It is a good thing I didn't go with you, although I promise I'd rather be there. It is going to take some rebuilding and some time to get the place back up and running. When are you coming back home anyway?" That was something they hadn't really discussed because he was going with her and it originally didn't make a difference, but now, he didn't want to be without her for too long.

Taking in a deep breath, "I am not really sure. Hopefully within a few weeks. That way you have time to get your restaurant back on track also." She knew he could care less about the business. She heard someone calling him in the background and used that to help get off the phone. Charisma said her goodbyes and told him she would call him later that evening once she settled in.

Once she finished gathering her luggage and was heading to the exit, she saw a face she would never forget. It was Olivia's face, but in a smaller version. Olivia told her she had children, but it hadn't really sunk in until that moment. Looking beside the little girl, who had to be about 7, there was a little version of Jackson, he had to be about 5. Charisma's mouth dropped. The children were gorgeous and looked just like her friends did when they were younger.

After the initial shock, she saw Livia, but there was no Jackson. Charisma hugged Olivia and neither of the friends wanted to let the other go.

"Mommy, Mommy, is that Auntie Risma?"

Smiling harder than she had smiled in quite some time, Livia replied, "yes my love, this is her. She finally came home. This is Mommy's best friend in the whole wide world, next to Daddy of course." Olivia felt Charisma's eyes burning through her at that moment. "Yes Risma, I know, you have questions and you want answers. Well so do I, just so you know. Now, Charleigh-Rose and Little Jack this is your auntie."

The children both smiled and hugged Charisma as if they had known her for years. Charisma looked confused by Olivia's comment, and then remembered she was supposed to have been bringing Tyrese.

"Really Liv, I only told you about that right before I was about to board the plane. Things have changed since then. An emergency came up at work." That was a big deal for Charisma, and Olivia knew it. She had never imagined coming back home, much less bringing a guy with her. Olivia couldn't wait to hear all about him and to find out why he didn't come with her.

The whole drive to Olivia's, Charleigh-Rose was talking Charisma's ear off, while Jack just stared at her.

"Where have you been? Mommy talks about you all the time. Do you have children like me and Jack? Are you married like Mommy and Daddy? Are you coming to live with us? Mommy said you don't have any family besides her and Dad, is that true?" Before Charisma could answer the first question, the inquisitive child had asked 10 more. Laughing to herself, Charisma remembered how Livia was around that age. Even in class she was always raising her hand to ask the teacher questions. Looks like the apple didn't fall too far away from the tree at all.

As they were pulling up to Olivia's home, Charisma's phone rang. She knew it was Tyrese. Without even looking at the caller id display, she answered, "Yes Tyrese, I am okaaaaaaaaaaaaaaayyyyy."

The voice on the other end of the phone, stuttered a bit, "ex... excuse me? My apologies ma'am but my name isn't Tyrese, but it is great to know you are okay."

Immediately Charisma was embarrassed. "I'm sorry, let's try this again. Who are you and what can I help you with?"

she could hear the guy smiling through the phone. "Yes ma'am, my name is Delton Morris, and I am the attorney handling your mother's estate. I have been trying to contact you for some time. She was trying to get things in order prior to her taking ill."

Charisma wanted to correct him and tell him Ms. Beatrice wasn't her mom, but in her heart, she knew she was indeed the closest thing that she ever had after her own mother passed. Even though Ms. Beatrice never reached out to her, Charisma knew she was aware of where she was living. For her birthdays and holidays, she always received cards unsigned.

"Sir, you must be mistaken, my mother didn't have an estate. At least none that I ever knew about. She always seemed to be struggling on her social security and the money she received from the state for me."

Delton hesitated for a moment, "that is unfortunate. Such a kind lady struggling financially is not good at all. The reason for the call is to inquire if you were going to be present for her funeral and the reading of the will?"

Charisma was taken back by his straightforwardness. "Mr. Delton, was it? I literally just landed here in Iowa and yes, I have been made aware that the funeral is tomorrow, and the will is to be read later tomorrow around 5 pm. Is that all correct?"

Delton smiled to himself. Ms. Beatrice always told him that Charisma was a bit of a firecracker and now he could see just what she meant. "Yes ma'am, you seem to have it all together. I will leave you to it then and I will see you tomorrow."

Charisma wanted so badly to catch up with Olivia about all that was going on with her and Jackson over these last fifteen years. But she was so exhausted between the flight, the thought of dealing with Ms. Beatrice's affairs, the ones that she knew nothing of. She picked up her phone to call Tyrese, and she realized she had missed two calls from him and a message. Dialing his number, she gathered herself, the phone rang and he picked up on the third ring.

"Hey baby," he said into the phone.

She smiled. "Hey, is everything okay Tyrese? I see I missed your calls and a message."

"Yeah, I was just calling to make sure you were okay, and to tell you that I will be there just as soon as I get this mess straightened out, unless you are back home by then. At least I'm hoping you will be home by then. I miss you already Char."

She had to admit to herself, she missed him a little too. It was reassuring to know he was right there even when she acted like she didn't want him to be. "I miss you too Rese, but I will be home before you know it. I need to wrap things up here and I will be on my way. I do want to hang out with my niece and nephew for a week or so though to get to know them. They are amazing and nosey. Wish I had been around them more, so they would know me, and I them. But, no worries, we are going to make up for lost time."

Tyrese smiled to himself, this was a nice side to see of his lady. One that he hadn't seen before that is for sure. She usually guarded herself against personal attachments but for some reason with these children she welcomed it. That gave Tyrese room to hope that maybe she would eventually come around and marry him and perhaps start a family of their own one day soon. "Take your time Char, but just not too much time. I don't want you to forget about me."

Charisma laughed out loud, "Tyrese, I would never forget about you, no matter what. You have nothing to worry about. I promise you that. So please stop worrying, okay? Can you do that for me? Because I cannot handle my business here while I'm worrying about you there. I know we haven't been apart for a long time before, but babe, I will be back sooner than you realize."

Tyrese smiled through the phone and he genuinely felt better. "Enjoy your friends Char and just know that I love you and miss you."

In Charisma's head she was thinking *there he goes saying that again. Maybe I should just tell him that I love him too? Perhaps he will feel better.*

Almost as if reading her thoughts Tyrese interrupted her mental discussion with herself. "Charisma, I didn't say it for you to feel forced into saying it back. We have been over this. It will come in time. I am sure of that."

With a long sigh, Charisma told him she needed to go but that they would talk soon. She told him she missed him and couldn't wait to be home again. Which was all true by the way. One day she would admit it to him that she loved him, just maybe not right this minute.

Hanging up the phone she was still amazed that he hadn't brought up the fact of using the l word. *Maybe he is a keeper. I still don't know why he is so patient with me. Any other man would have left a long time ago. Any woman would be happy to have him all over them. What is wrong with me? Maybe after this trip I will wake up and realize just what I do have in Rese.* Truth be told if it were the other way around, she would have left him alone.

Picking up her phone she dialed Tyrese's number back because she realized she hadn't told him the funeral was tomorrow and so was the reading of the will. She didn't want him getting worried if she didn't answer the phone or respond to his messages for long periods of time. When she heard the phone was answered she began to talk without awaiting a hello. "Babe, listen, I forgot to tell you tomorrow is going to be pretty busy and a little crazy so it may not be until late...Babe?"

a woman's voice replied to Charisma's. "Hello, I'm sorry, Ty can't come to the phone right now. Is there something I can help you with?"

Charisma had to gather her thoughts for a moment, did a woman just answer Tyrese's phone? She doesn't even do that.

Just as she was about to reply, she heard Tyrese's voice "Sahara, give me the phone." As soon as Tyrese got on the phone, "Char, what's wrong?"

Charisma immediately fired back, "what do you mean, what's wrong? So, I can't call you back now? Really Rese, I haven't been gone a whole day yet, or was this going on before I left?"

In their whole time together, Tyrese had never heard or seen her act that way. On the inside Tyrese was loving the fact that she had just laid her cards on the table, even if Char didn't realize it. The jealousy was something he wasn't used to. He had come accustomed to seeing her spicy side a time or two in the past. He knew it was best to let her get it out of her system before trying to reason with her. Patiently he waited for her to finish and when she did, he spoke up. "Char, nothing is going on here. You know you can call me at any time, no matter the time of day. I have nothing to hide. Are you calm enough for me to explain who she is?" when he received no reply, he continued. "Sahara is my sister, she just got into town a little bit ago from London, and I was going to tell you when we spoke tomorrow. She heard about the fire and she was worried, so she came to check in on me and lend a hand if needed. She has been contemplating moving to the states for a while now. So, while she's here she is looking for places. Char, Char say something please."

All the while he was explaining Charisma was starting to feel like a complete idiot. There was just so much going on in her world and it wasn't something she was used to. She always prided herself on being able to handle any obstacles life threw at her and knowing what was going on and when in her life. For one of the first times in her adult life, it was in utter chaos. She mumbled, "I apologize babe. I just got upset, I don't even answer your phone. It just took me by surprise, that's all."

Again, Tyrese got another inkling the woman he loved was a human being. For the first time she was exposed and vulnerable and he was trying to be understanding and tread lightly to not take advantage of her. God, he loved her. "Babe hang up the phone, I'm going to video call you, so I can introduce you two. It is about time you two have met anyway."

Doing as she was told she pressed the call end button. The phone immediately rang back. Answering she smiled into the phone, "Hello babe, I'm here." Looking into the phone she could see a female version of her guy. This woman that he was introducing was simply gorgeous. She had the same eyes and complexion as her brother, and when she smiled, Charisma couldn't help but smile back. There was no denying they were siblings.

"Sahara this is my Char, Char my love, this is my other half Sahara, well she was until you came along." Giving his sister the side eye.

Sahara chimed in, "Hello love, it is a pleasure to meet you. Sorry it is under these circumstances. I hated to hear about your mum and then with Ty being stuck here. If he gets me caught up on what needs to be done around here I may be able to get him to you soon. I'm sure he would like that; however, you may require a holiday away from him."

Laughing, Charisma shook her head no. "It is a pleasure to

meet you also. It would be great if he were able to get here, but I know how important his restaurant is to him."

In the background, Tyrese shouted "You are more important, you know that Char, but we will see what happens."

Grabbing the phone back from his sister, "now what was it love that you wanted to talk about before all of those shenanigans?"

Still feeling embarrassed, Charisma told him about the call from the lawyer and the funeral was going to be at noon, and then she was to meet the lawyer at five o'clock for the reading of the will. She told him she had no idea as to what to expect but she wanted him to know that it may be late before she was able to contact him. He really didn't like it, but he understood, he told her he would be there when she needed him. Even as she told him this, she had no idea just what she was in for tomorrow. She prayed it would be easy, after all she had never even attended a funeral before, thankfully she didn't have to plan it. That would have been a disaster, almost how this call started out. She was glad she was wrong; she didn't want to believe that Tyrese was just like all the others. So far, he has been more than she could have ever hoped for.

As Charisma was settling in on the bed, she heard a knock and then the door suddenly burst open. She was immediately bombarded by two adults and two minions. Everyone seemed to dive onto the bed simultaneously, she could only smile and laugh. She laughed harder than she had in quite some time. Her mind went back to when she, Liv and Jackson were younger and them doing this exact same thing.

Ms. Beatrice used to tell them all the time, "you break it, you bought it." She never really fussed at Charisma or her friends. Boy things were different when they were at Liv's house though, her parents were mean.

You couldn't move without getting in trouble. "Stop stomping in my house. Stop playing so much. Go outside with that nonsense," her dad would always yell, he worked the night shift, so he was always trying to sleep during the day.

They didn't care though, they were just having fun, and they would pack up and go to Ms. Beatrice's house. Charisma had never really felt that Ms. Beatrice was always there, once she was placed with her. This was where she felt the safest. She knew if she needed her, she would be there. Liv and Jackson realized it back when they were children, even when Charisma didn't. Things weren't bad, she didn't have to worry about being accused of being hot in the pants, or even the fact of not being believed. Ms. Beatrice always had her back. She was quick to let people know she was with her. Thinking back Ms. Beatrice claimed her long before she did.

7

BACK TOGETHER AGAIN

Jackson gave Charisma the biggest hug ever. "Oh, my god, look at you. How I have missed you. Glad to finally lay eyes on you again. We have been so worried about you through the years. But I must say New Orleans agrees with you."

Olivia agreed with Jackson.

"I think it was good for you to get away and start over. I just wish you hadn't stayed away for so long. We have missed you so much."

As tears began to roll down Charisma's face, she replied solemnly, "I've missed you guys too. I see I have missed out on a lot." She looked over at the children. They had gotten comfortable and were just about asleep. They were a beautiful combination of her best friends.

"So, what is it like, this whole parenting thing? If they are anything like you two were, it can't be easy." Charisma smiled as she teased her friends.

Livia was the first to chime in, "nothing like I thought it would be. I just knew I didn't want to repeat what any of us went through as children. I strive every day to give them the love and foundation they need. Jackson handles everything else."

"Yeah, she took the easy part. You know Risma, none of us had it easy, least of all you, we are just trying to provide better for our kids, so they don't ever have to know that world from which we came from." Both Liv and Jackson had come from abusive families. Jackson's father would punch on his mom as if she was a punching bag. He eventually started hitting Jackson too. His father thought it would make him tough like a man should be. Liv's mom was always drinking or popping whatever the new fad pill was at the time. She would take her frustrations out on her two daughters, by not feeding them. Liv was told more than a few times that she wasn't going to amount to anything. She began to believe it. Liv's dad was the only one who could handle her mom. When he was shot and killed in a robbery at the bank he worked at, it was open season on the girls.

"They know who you are and what you mean to us. They even know, there would be no Mommy and Daddy if it wasn't for you. When you left, Liv's and my bond became tighter. We had to rely on each other to get through our individual storms. There is so much to catch you up on. But for tonight we are going to revel in the fact you are home. Get some rest my friend, we have a long day tomorrow, we have your three and your nine. The children have your six."

She couldn't believe this guy talking was Jackson, the same knucklehead that used to follow her around. He was somebody's father, husband, and still her best friend.

Jackson looked over at the children, "Oh yeah, they can fall out anywhere. Just like me."

"Please let them stay in here with me tonight, if they will." Charisma surprised herself with her own request. Livia, who had been quietly taking this all in, smiled to herself, and knew that her friend was glad to be home, even if there was a lot of painful memories here. There was also some good coming from it.

"Alright Risma, get some rest, early day and a long one ahead tomorrow. Jackson and I are in the room across the hall if you need anything. I love you and I am so glad you are back, even if it is only for a short time."

Charisma's eyes were closed before her head hit the pillow. She was beyond exhausted. After a few hours, she felt someone starring at her. When she opened her eyes, sure enough Charleigh-Rose was two inches from her face, so close, she felt every breath.

When she opened her eyes, she startled the little girl for a second. "You snore when you sleep. Daddy says that means you have worked hard. Did you work hard yesterday before you got here Auntie, because you were snoring really, really, really loudly?"

Charisma could only smile and nod yes. This seemed to have satisfied Charleigh. Risma did not want to be the one to destroy a daughter and father's trust over something as innocuous as snoring.

When the alarm sounded from her phone, Charisma tried to ignore it. She had purposely put it on that annoying escalating tone for just such occasions. Morning came all too suddenly and she honestly wasn't prepared for what the day would bring. To act as if Ms. Beatrice didn't really matter to her, seemed to have helped her prior to this moment and was her defense mechanism. Truth was, she welcomed the cards that she had received through the years. It was a reminder that she wasn't truly alone. She tried to not look forward to them because she knew they would eventually stop. With each one her face would light up betraying her true emotions. Charisma thought Ms. Beatrice would get tired of sending them, she had never really contemplated her death. Somewhere in the back of her mind she always knew if she had to, she could return home and Ms.

Beatrice would welcome her as she did that first day so many years before. So many memories began to flood her thoughts. Charisma felt her heart ache at the thought of what today meant.

To clear her thoughts, she decided to take a shower. Thinking that this would help, it only seemed to bring forward more memories of a time long ago. A welcome intrusion came about fifteen minutes into the shower when there was a knock on the bathroom door.

"Yes," she called out. To her surprise in comes little Jackson, heading straight for the commode. Either he didn't know she was there, or he just didn't care. She pulled her towel from the hook next to the shower to cover herself quickly when she heard the door opening. Charisma realized that he was sleep-walking, but he did well to wash his hands. She couldn't help but smile, he did the whole process with his eyes closed. When he left out, she dried herself and dressed. She went and peeked in LJ's bed he wasn't there, but he was back in her bed.

Smiling to herself, she went to see if anyone else was awake yet. No one was moving about but the time was winding down. She imagined Charleigh-Rose was still sleeping, because of her late-night visit with Risma. In the middle of getting dressed she heard Liv outside of the door, "I'm coming in, I hope you are awake."

"Are you actually giving me a warning? You must have gotten soft in your old age. I remember you would just simply barge in on me. Both you and Jackson would, like it was nothing. Thanks for the warning."

Liv entered the room, laughing, "hey by the way, did you have company when you were showering this morning?"

"Yeah Jackson, well LJ paid me a visit. Is that normal for him?"

Olivia nodded her head yes. Apparently the doctors had told her that eventually he might grow out of it. She was just thankful that he didn't leave a mess when he did it. She had narrowed it down, only when he is super excited, was when it occurs. He had been excited that Charisma was there, although he spent most of his time just watching her. It was obvious that he was captivated by her beauty just like his dad had been years ago, but he decided on another route.

8

NOT PREPARED

Ms. Beatrice was a meticulous planner; thankfully she had taken care of all the arrangements for her funeral. Charisma was glad about that because if it was up to her, Ms. Beatrice may have been buried in a plain ol' pine box, about two feet in the ground. Charisma wouldn't have known where to start. She had never been to a funeral or a wedding in her entire life. Her limited knowledge came from what she saw on television or in the movies.

Ms. Beatrice had opted to have a small memorial service at the funeral home. When Charisma entered the room, she was lucky there was reserved seating for her, Liv, Jackson, and the children. Otherwise she would have been standing with the other fifteen or so who were standing in the back determined to pay their respects to Ms. Beatrice. She was well loved in the small community. Alonzo and his wife Natasha were there, they ran the bakery downtown. They had always sent her fresh bread and deserts. Their lemon meringue pie was to die for. Looking around she noticed BJ the mechanic was there. He owned a small family auto body shop and did most of the mechanic work for the neighborhood. He was a godsend to those who could not afford the more expensive dealerships cost for repairs. Charisma saw several others that she immediately recognized, it was almost as if time stood still for most of them. Joe the barber greeted her with a hug. His barbershop had saved her a time or two when she was trying to hide away from her foster families. He had a daughter Sophia who Charisma used to like. They played hopscotch, jumped double-dutch together, and would often sneak candy from the corner store. Although it wasn't much of a sneak, Mr. Johnson knew what they were doing. He never said anything, he always thought they could be doing worse.

So many memories were flooding her mind. Charisma thought to herself, she should have come by to see Ms. Beatrice yesterday when she first arrived. She did look beautiful. They had her laying there as if she was merely sleeping. Charisma noticed that her hair was up in the back, and for the first time she noticed, Ms. Beatrice had a streak of gold hair at the base of her neck as well. This caught her off guard and she stumbled back slightly. There to brace her was, Delton Morris, since she hadn't met him, she just thought he was a random person. She gathered herself and thanked the gentleman. Charisma found her seat beside Olivia. Leaning in Liv asked her if she was okay. She simply nodded. Charisma was anything but okay though, the gold hairs threw her. After doing some research about it in high school, she knew that it wasn't a common thing, but what does it mean? She was deep in thought when the preacher called her up to say a few words. Liv had to tap her out of her daydream. She began panicking, she had not prepared anything, she didn't realize she had to speak. This was becoming more and more complicated by the moment.

Stepping up to the front of the room, she took a deep breath before she began to tell of the kind lady who took her in. She spoke of Ms. Beatrice with actual affection. "As a child back then, I thought everybody was out for just a check, or to take advantage of those who needed a home. My thoughts were to always just bide my time and cause as little uproar for the family as possible. Sometimes it worked, others it did not. By the time I was placed with Ms. Beatrice, I won't lie, I had been through some things, and no one seemed to understand or even believe me. Except Ms. Beatrice, and my two best friends. I can still remember the first day I was with her; she told me that I would never have to worry about anything or anyone harming me ever again. As I am speaking to you all now, I am just swimming in the memories that have come crashing over me since I returned to town. Ms. Beatrice was like a mother or a granny to me, and she always beamed with delight when people said we favored. She was an amazing woman, but all of you know that. I am thankful that she took me in when she did, and even though I left she always knew where I was and let me know it in her own way. Today I honor her as my mother." Charisma had been getting choked up throughout her whole speech, and she found it too hard to hold back the tears any longer. As they began flowing, her eyes found Liv, and she came for her and guided her back to her seat. She whispered a "I love you." Olivia knew that this was going to be hard on her friend, but she didn't know it would break her down this much. Throughout the rest of the service, she prayed that God would give her friend the strength to endure. Sometimes until things are gone, we never truly understand what they meant to us or how crucial they were to how we arrived at our current place. As the mourners came up to show their respect, some displayed their grief more than others. BJ, Alonzo, and his wife showed out the most. Alonzo's wife Phyllis laid across Ms. Beatrice's casket, and sobbed her eyes out.

After the service, Charisma wasn't really in the mood to attend the reading of the will. She had been shaken up more than even she would like to admit. It was just something about knowing, if she ever truly needed to come back, Ms. Beatrice would be there with open arms. And now that safety net was gone, she would never again be able to walk in the front door of Ms. Beatrice's and be welcomed with a glass of sweet tea. Truthfully, she never thought she would feel that way about anyone especially since her mother had passed. She asked Liv to take her back to the house, so she could get a little rest before going to see the lawyer. Liv didn't protest. She knew her friend was dealt a rough blow today.

"Listen girly, you know you have to pull yourself together. It is almost over. Jackson and I are here for you, and always will be. We love you Risma."

Before she could get her eyes closed good, Charleigh–Rose was waking her up. She wasn't prepared for what happened at the service, but she felt confident the reading of the will would be easier to handle. It had to be less emotional. Besides, she still didn't believe Ms. Beatrice had any affairs that required a lawyer to begin with.

Just then, in burst Jackson, and right on his heels was Liv. "Alright girl, are you ready to go and put this all behind you so we can focus on the fun we going to have later tonight?"

Side eyeing Liv, she shook her head no. Of course, she was ready to get it over with, but not for any fun. She couldn't deny the fact that she had a few questions now, that she had never thought about before. Charisma hadn't had the chance to tell Liv about the gold hair that she had seen on the nape of Ms. Beatrice's neck. Charisma made up in her mind they would talk later that evening, after the kids went to bed.

When Charisma arrived at the lawyer's office she was quickly greeted by a petite and overly friendly secretary, who said her name was Ginger. Standing inside the doorway she was being ushered into was the man who had steadied her at the service earlier.

He interrupted her thoughts and stepped forward and extended his hand to her as she walked into the room. "I wish time had allowed us to meet prior to this morning, but sometimes things can't be avoided."

Charisma simply smiled. "Mr. Delton, was it? It is a pleasure to meet you. Now that I am here, can we get on with this dealing with her affairs so that I can get back home." Ms. Beatrice had warned him time and again just how standoffish this one was.

He smirked and took a little pleasure in letting her know, "Miss Charisma, I do apologize for any inconvenience that Ms. Beatrice's untimely departure has had in your life, but we are waiting on a few others to arrive. You are more than welcome to take your seat inside. They should be here shortly, as you are here a few minutes early." He turned and walked away without allowing her to speak another word. Delton knew that would get to her. He smiled to himself.

Taking a seat, Charisma positioned herself so that she could see as the others slowly began to enter in. The first to arrive was Alonzo and his wife. She had so many fond memories of them and their bakery. They were guaranteed fresh desserts at least once a week if not more. Next BJ and Joe came in talking to each other, with Mr. Johnson following closely behind. As everyone walked in, they looked Charisma's way with uncertainty in their eyes. Charisma couldn't fathom that the businesses these kind people owned somehow belonged to Ms. Beatrice. Her mind began spinning and racing out of control, just then she saw a young lady enter the room perhaps a little older than she herself, but she wasn't alone. Charisma's eyes quickly darted down to the stroller she was pushing. This lady, Charisma didn't recognize, and she wanted to ask Liv for some help to figure it out, but she was out of reach. When they arrived Liv and Jackson went in and found some seats. The seats were on the opposite side from where Risma was ushered to. As if on cue, Liv looked in Charisma's direction. Their eyes connected and then looked at the lady and back again to each other. Liv shrugged her shoulders. She hadn't seen the lady around town. She couldn't offer any answers as to the mysterious new arrival.

Some of the guys were still standing, while others were beginning to sit. Delton must have decided it was time to begin.

Clearing his throat, "Can I have everyone's attention please. If everyone would go ahead and be seated, we can proceed. I do believe that everyone is finally here."

Looking around the room, his gaze steadied on Charisma. Goodness she was just beautiful. He saw pictures of her from when she was younger, and she was a looker then, but she could make a man get caught up in his feelings if he wasn't careful now.

Snapping himself back into focus. Looking down at the documents on the table and remembering why they were gathered there to begin with. "Ms. Beatrice wanted you all present here today for the reading of her last will and testament. For some of you this will be a shock, and others it will not be." He began reading off the document to the group and most seemed happy with what was read. Charisma just listened in awe. It seemed that all these years Ms. Beatrice owned the bakery, barbershop, corner store, and mechanic shop. In her will, she left it to each of the owners with the exception that they each gave Charisma either five thousand or one hundred per month as they had been giving her through the remaining ten-year term on their lease. They all agreed to the five thousand. "To my beloved Charisma, I leave the monies from the businesses mentioned earlier as stated. I also leave you our home in which you may do with as you wish. There is an envelope addressed to you, with some important documents that you will need to read when you are alone. There is so much I never had the chance to share with you. Delton will take care of all the business affairs for you and ensure that whatever arrangements need to be made are made timely. I tried to make this short and sweet, I love you and always have." Just as quickly as he had begun reading, he was done.

Everyone began standing and coming around towards Charisma to hug her and offer her their condolences and tell her they would get her their checks within the coming days. Charisma realized everyone seemed to have been acknowledged except the woman and the child.

9

REALITY SETS IN

Delton asked for Charisma to stay back so of course Liv and Jackson weren't leaving without her. She noticed that he had motioned for the mother to stay back as well. As soon as the others left, his secretary locked the door.

Delton introduced Charisma to the mystery lady. "Elaina this is Charisma, Charisma this is Elaina, she is a friend of your dad's."

Charisma looked confused. "I don't have a father." Charisma almost yelled. She stood there with almost a look of pure disgust.

Delton intervened from the front of the room, "Look at the child Charisma. Look at the back of her head. It is obvious. It is a signature so to speak."

Charisma just shook her head. "What are you saying? Is this child is related to me? Ms. Beatrice is related to me? My dad is Ms. Beatrice son? What is it?"

Delton answered her questions, "I am afraid all of it. I know it is a hard pill to swallow especially now. Ms. Beatrice wasn't sure. She didn't know for certain until a few years ago. But you had already made your choice to leave and she didn't want to disrupt your life. Here is the letter. You can read it now or take it with you, but we have to make some decisions really soon." Delton hated to have to deliver this message to her, there were other things that Charisma had no idea of that made this a sticky situation.

Charisma practically snatched the letter from him. She looked up at him apologetically as she realized how she must look. "I'm sorry. I'm sure that this isn't something you wanted to be involved in. Please forgive my abrasive attitude." It wasn't his fault. Inside she was boiling with confusion and anger and heartbreak. A dad, a sibling, a grandmother all at one time. All this time she thought she was alone, but she wasn't. But in an instant, she was again. Well not totally, there was this child. What was she supposed to do with this child?

She opened the letter, *My dearest Charisma, this isn't the way I would have wanted to tell you any of this, but I have no choice in the matter. As you can guess by now, I am your biological grandmother. This information, I only discovered a few years ago myself. I had always had my suspicions, but I thought it was the wishful desires of an old lady. I hired some people to do some digging and turns out, it is true. You did belong to me after all. My only regret is that I would have known it sooner and had more time with you. Your father chose to leave my home and run in the life, dealing drugs and living in and out of jail. It is funny how life comes full circle and brings people back together. I never knew you existed until you had left me too. Elaina has been caring for Tia, your little sister, since she was born eight months ago. Her mother was using drugs along with your father at the time of her birth. There was a car accident and they both died. He died instantly, and she shortly after giving birth. Tia was meant to be here. I would have taken her in myself, but my health began failing me in the worst way. I have made the necessary provisions to provide financially for both of my granddaughters for the bulk of your lives. I only wish I could do more. I know money doesn't replace time or the family you never knew you had, but I hope that it helps to make your life a little easier. I have always been proud of what you have been able to accomplish with the cards you have been dealt in life. I truly believe that you can be a positive influence over your sister's life. She needs you as much as you need her.* Her eyes swelled with tears as she read the words, she could hear Ms. Beatrice's voice speaking to her softly. She longed for the days when she would hug her tight and tell her it would be all right, no matter how much of a tough girl act she attempted to play. She knew no matter what she was always there. Until she wasn't. She had the best advice and it was always spot on. Charisma sure could use some of that advice now. So many thoughts flooded her mind. How was she going to raise a child? Oh, my god, what about Tyrese? She hadn't even thought about Tyrese during this whole thing. What is he going to think? What is he going to say? They never talked about having a family or any of this. More importantly, she wasn't ready to raise a child, she had no idea how to. Just then Tia began to cry, disrupting her thoughts snapping her back into reality, her new reality whether she wanted it or not.

Tears began flooding her eyes, she looked over to Liv helplessly, who ran immediately to her side. Just then she collapsed to the floor with a loud thud. Jackson tried to get to her just as Liv reached for her. They both missed and ended up grabbing each other.

Bending down immediately they lift her head up and check for blood or swelling. Jackson exhaled harshly, *thank god there is no blood. He also noticed no immediate swelling.* Charisma had been out for a few minutes, but it seemed like an eternity to her friends.

Liv began calling her name, "Risma, Risma, wake up sweetie. Please wake up." Liv was gently shaking her at the same time.

Charisma started stirring, moaning as she tried to sit up. She immediately touched the back of her head. "What happened?"

53

She asked. Looking at her friends kneeling around her, even Delton was standing above her with a glass of water.

No one spoke up in response to Charisma. She started to try and stand so she could get to one of the chairs.

"Take your time Risma," Liv stated.

Once she got to the chair, she looked to her friends for answers. She accepted the glass of water from Delton, she noticed that color was finally returning to his face.

Delton was the first to speak, "Charisma, again I know this is a bit much for you to digest. To put this as simply as I can, your grandmother, God rest her soul was a saint. She did so much for so many people and never asked for much in return. You do have some financial decisions to make, and I will be here to help you through most of them. The one thing, which I can't help you with, is the baby. Your sister Tia, in my opinion deserves to know that she isn't alone in this world." Delton paused as he watched Charisma's facial expression. Her mouth was open wide, if a fly was around; it surely would have landed in her mouth. That he was sure of.

Just then Tia began to cry, for a bit it seemed that she was forgotten. Charisma looked over at her sister. *Her sister.* How was she going to raise a child, she didn't have a role model to follow.

As if reading her mind, Delton jumped in. "Just remember the kindness and love that Ms. Beatrice showed you. She didn't even know you were her grandchild, but she gave you the love you didn't even know you needed."

Charisma agreed by shaking her head and cutting her eyes to Liv and Jackson. "Yes of course, we will always be here to help you. No matter what, we love you kiddo."

Jackson agreed with his wife. "You have so much love to give, you just don't know it. Besides you know what not to do."

Charisma's thoughts flashed to Tyrese. *Omg, what is he going to think? What if this is too much for him? I know he loves me, but now with a kid to take care of? Even I would walk away from me.* Just then her phone rang.

"Char, are you okay baby? I was trying to be patient and wait for your call to tell me how everything went."

When Tyrese stopped for a breather, Charisma jumped in. "Tyrese there is so much going on here. I'm still at the attorney's office. I promise I will call you tonight."

There was something in her voice, if Tyrese didn't know anything else, he paid close attention to this woman that he loved. "Baby, what is it? Can't you step outside for just a minute so we can talk?"

Charisma stood strong, even though she was still feeling a little weak and lightheaded from the fall. "Tye let me call you in a bit please."

Tyrese knew when to back down. "Ok babe make sure you call me tonight. I feel like there is something wrong." She agreed and hung up the phone.

Taking a deep breath, she turned back to her friends. "Can we go please?" Delton walked them out to the car, he was carrying Tia in his arms, while Jackson had the car seat with the stroller connected. Liv was walking arm in arm with Charisma. Once they reached the car, Jackson folded the stroller up and placed it in the trunk. The car seat he strapped into the back seat.

How does he know how to do this so quickly?

Charisma got into the back seat as Delton strapped Tia in. Elaina ran out behind them carrying the diaper bag and suit-case, which Charisma assumed had her clothes, and other belongings in it. Jackson placed those items in the trunk. As Jackson and Liv got into the car, Charisma couldn't help but look over at Tia. Her patch of golden hair was more prominent than Charisma's. Tia smiled as she released some gas. Her smile turned into a giggle.

There was no denying that giggle even in this small body was Ms. Beatrice all day long.

That warmed Charisma's heart where this little one was concerned. Charisma began playing with Tia's fingers and the little girl latched on and wouldn't let go until they were ready to get out of the car.

10

NO LONGER ALONE

The children ran to the car when Liv, Jackson, Charisma, and baby Tia arrived home. The babysitter Anya, trotted out behind them, yelling their names.

The children kept running. "Mommy, Mommy, Daddyyyyy…" the two of them took turns yelling. The two of them got wide eyed when they saw the baby in the back with Charisma.

Charleigh-Rose was the first to speak, "Auntie Risma, you have a baby. Can I hold her?"

Jackson spoke up quickly derailing his daughter's incessant need for answers, "maybe when we get inside little one."

Charisma smiled as she unstrapped Tia successfully by herself. *Maybe she wouldn't be as bad at this as she thought.*

Since getting off the phone a few hours ago, Tyrese had been pacing the floor as his sister looked on.

"When does the flight leave? What can I do?" knowing her brother all too well, they spoke at the same time, "Nothing."

Sahara smiled, it was times like this, that made her feel close to her brother.

"There is something wrong and I don't know what to do?

What if I go and she doesn't want me there? What will I do Sahara?"

walking over to her brother, she hugged him tight. "Go be with her, I will handle stuff here. She is more important. Don't make the mistakes I have." Sahara was referring to her last relationship with an actor. She chose to be alone instead of fighting to be with him. That was one of the reasons she was here now with Tyrese. She needed to be with her brother and regroup.

"Alright Sis, my flight leaves in an hour. Do you mind dropping me at the airport? I really don't want to leave the car in long-term parking. Not sure how soon I will be back."

Sahara grabbed her keys and was heading to the door before he finished the whole question.

Charisma was drained after today's activities. She knew she was supposed to call Tyrese. She just didn't have it in her. He was going to ask her questions she wasn't sure she would be able to answer. Thankfully Tia was a good baby. Liv, helped to get her fed, changed, bathed, and finally to sleep. Liv had LJ's crib put back together within 30 minutes. Risma was grateful to Jackson for his running interference with the children's questions. She wasn't ready for that either. Her mind finally calmed down and she dozed off to sleep.

When she woke up a few hours later she saw there was a missed call from Tyrese. It was too late to call him back. With a quick check on Tia, a few minutes later she was asleep again.

The next time she woke up, she heard someone calling her name. She had to be dreaming, there was no way that Tye was here. As she opened her eyes fully, she saw him on his knees beside the bed. Charisma sat straight up in the bed and looked over at the crib.

"Hey Char, I know all about what happened."

Charisma was still confused. "How did you get here? Why are you here?" Immediately she regretted saying it like that. "I didn't mean it like that. Tye, I'm so happy that you are here."

Tyrese pulled her close, "I knew something was going on. I felt helpless. Sahara is taking care of things at home, until we get back." He could feel Risma as a smile crept to her face.

"You'd do that for me?"

Without a moment's hesitation he said, "of course. You have no idea how much I love you, do you? I told you I am here and would be here for you. All I'm waiting for is for you to say you want me too."

"Tyrese, I can't ask you to take on a baby. I don't even know what I'm doing."

"Char, the decision is made. Just tell me what you want?"

"I want you!"

"Finally!" Tyrese said and exhaled.

"I love you Risma."

"I love you too Tye, for always and forever."

Never did Charisma imagine she would be back in her hometown, raising a baby with a man she loved. Finally, she was no longer alone in this world, she has a sister, her best friends, and a soon to be husband.

AFTERWORD

Thank You for Reading….

Don't forget to sign up for
Mind Flow Publishing & Production LLC's Newsletter @ www.
mindflowpublishingproduction.com

Email us for autographed or additional paperback copies @
mindflowpubpro@gmail.com

Other Titles Also Available Include
Mental Interlude – Poetry
The Mary B Chronicles – Fiction
Journey to Living (Kindle only) – Inspirational
Simple Complexity -- Poetry
Spoken From The Heart – Poetry
Dreams Do Come True – Fiction

Available Through
Amazon
Barnes & Noble

Kindle

Coming Soon
For Her Love – Fiction
To Be Chosen – Paranormal Romance

The Hitchhiker — Fiction
A Prince For Me – Romantic Comedy
Forbidden – Romantic Suspense

Upcoming Titles Will Be Available Through
Amazon
Barnes & Noble
Kindle
Apple iBooks
Kobo

ABOUT THE AUTHOR

Although I'm still considered new to the publishing world, I have hit the ground running full speed ahead. In my first year, I was signed to Mind Flow Publishing & Production LLC, and I have published a total of 6 books. I have earned Amazon's Best Sellers Top 100 orange banner. My latest work Spoken From The Heart, captured the #1 new release banner for several weeks. My works are spread across several genres such as; Poetry, Inspirational, and Christian fiction. I will be trying my hand at cozy mysteries, romance, and sci-fi. My love for writing started when I was about 12, writing poetry and writing speeches for various oratorical contests. Inspiration for my craft is pulled from my own life experiences, as well as others. I have been featured on several podcasts, as well as Up and Coming Authors Newsletters. When I'm not writing, I love to design shadowboxes, and create personalized greeting cards. I have released my 3rd poetry book (Spoken from the Heart) in August 2019. I will be releasing a minimum of 2 novellas (For Her Love will be one of them) before the end of 2019. Current books available are The Mary B Chronicles 1 & 2, Mental Interlude, and Journey to Living, Simple Complexity, and Dreams Do Come True. All of which are available on Amazon, and www.mindflowpublishingproduction.com.

facebook.com/DaKiara18

twitter.com/DakiaraP

instagram.com/iamthelyte

UNTITLED

FB @DaKiara18
   IG iamthelyte
   Twitter @DakiaraP
   FB @MindFlowPub
   Email mindflowpubpro@gmail.com
   Website www.mindflowpublishingproduction.com